P9-CFS-843

Best Friends
Forever

BiNK & gollie

Best Friends Forever

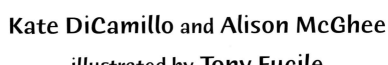

Kate DiCamillo and **Alison McGhee**

illustrated by **Tony Fucile**

CANDLEWICK PRESS

For Jennifer Roberts, tallest of them all

K. D.

For Charlie Anken, loved and missed

A. M.

For Stacey, my best friend forever

T. F.

Text copyright © 2013 by Kate DiCamillo and Alison McGhee
Illustrations copyright © 2013 by Tony Fucile

All rights reserved. No part of this book may be reproduced, transmitted, or stored
in an information retrieval system in any form or by any means, graphic, electronic, or
mechanical, including photocopying, taping, and recording, without prior written
permission from the publisher.

First edition 2013

Library of Congress Catalog Card Number 2012942669
ISBN 978-0-7636-3497-1

13 14 15 16 17 18 CCP 10 9 8 7 6 5 4 3 2 1

Printed in Shenzhen, Guangdong, China

This book was typeset in Humana Sans.
The illustrations were done digitally.

Candlewick Press
99 Dover Street
Somerville, Massachusetts 02144

visit us at www.candlewick.com

Contents

Empire
of
Enchantment

"I have long suspected that royal blood flowed in my veins," said Gollie.

Aunt Natasha
Sept. 21, 1908

"And here, at last, is the proof."

"Good news, Bink," said Gollie. "I have made an extraordinary discovery."

"I'll be right over," said Bink.

"Good news almost always means pancakes," said Bink.

"Bring on the pancakes," said Bink.

"Pancakes?" said Gollie. "What pancakes?"

"The good-news pancakes," said Bink.

"Bink," said Gollie, "you must stop thinking with your stomach. Look."

"Who's that?" said Bink.

"That," said Gollie, "is my great-aunt Natasha. As you
  can see, she was a queen."

"All righty, then," said Bink. "Let's eat!"

"I shall no longer be cooking pancakes for you, Bink,"
  said Gollie.

"Why not?" said Bink.

"I regret to inform you," said Gollie, "that royalty does not cook for others."

"Oh," said Bink. "Okay. I regret to inform you that I am going home."

"I look like my true self," said Gollie.

"The queen is thinking of paying you a visit, Bink," said Gollie.

"What queen?" said Bink.

"Queen Gollie," said Gollie.

"I'm not home," said Bink.

"Very well, then," said Gollie. "I shall go forth into my kingdom alone."

"A remarkable road," said Gollie.

"The queen thanks you for your efforts on behalf of the empire. Carry on."

"Lovely onions," said Gollie. "Pungent in the extreme.
The queen does love a good onion. Carry on."

"Mr. Eccles. Mrs. Eccles," said Gollie. "You may be interested to know that I, too, find myself in possession of an empire."

"May peace reign upon both of our empires," said Gollie.

"Knock, knock," said Gollie.

"Who's there?" said Bink.

"The queen," said Gollie.

"I'm still not home," said Bink.

"The Kingdom of Gollie has grown muddy," said Gollie.

"The crown grows heavy," said Gollie.

"The queen is lonely," said Gollie.

"Knock, knock," said Gollie.

"Who's there?" said Bink.

"It's me," said Gollie. "Gollie."

"Gollie," said Bink. "I've missed you."

Why
Should
You
Be
Shorter
Than
Your
Friends?

"Could you step aside, Bink?" said Gollie.

"I can reach that, Bink,"
said Gollie.

"Let me get that for you,
Bink," said Gollie.

"That's a good question," said Bink.

Why shouldn't you be tall?

PLACE
ORDER

"I can't think of a reason," said Bink.

PLACE YOUR
ORDER NOW

Name ....
Address ....

"All righty, then,"
said Bink. "I will."

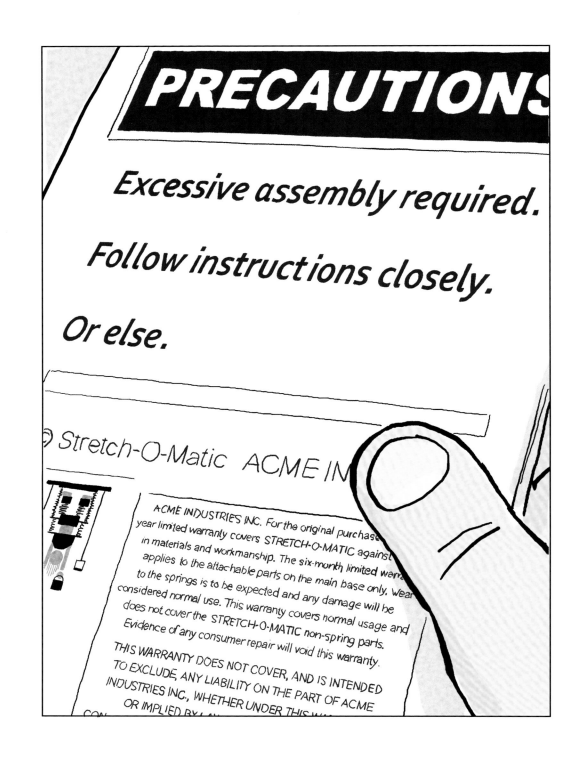

PRECAUTIONS

Excessive assembly required.

Follow instructions closely.

Or else.

© Stretch-O-Matic ACME IN

ACME INDUSTRIES INC. For the original purchase
year limited warranty covers STRETCH-O-MATIC against
in materials and workmanship. The six-month limited warra
applies to the attachable parts on the main base only. Wear
to the springs is to be expected and any damage will be
considered normal use. This warranty covers normal usage and
does not cover the STRETCH-O-MATIC non-spring parts.
Evidence of any consumer repair will void this warranty.

THIS WARRANTY DOES NOT COVER, AND IS INTENDED
TO EXCLUDE, ANY LIABILITY ON THE PART OF ACME
INDUSTRIES INC., WHETHER UNDER THIS W
OR IMPLIED BY LA

"Or else what?" said Bink.

"This Acme Stretch-o-Matic is top quality," said Bink.
"I can feel it working already."

KNOCK,
KNOCK,
KNOCK!

"Hello, Gollie," said Bink. "Notice anything different about me?"

"I do not," said Gollie.

"All righty, then," said Bink. "Back to the
 Acme Stretch-o-Matic."

"The Acme Stretch-o-Matic?"
said Gollie.

"Things are happening now,"
said Bink.

"Are you ready to be astonished, Gollie?" said Bink. "A dramatic change has occurred. You won't want to miss this. Act now!"

"Oh, dear," said Gollie.

47

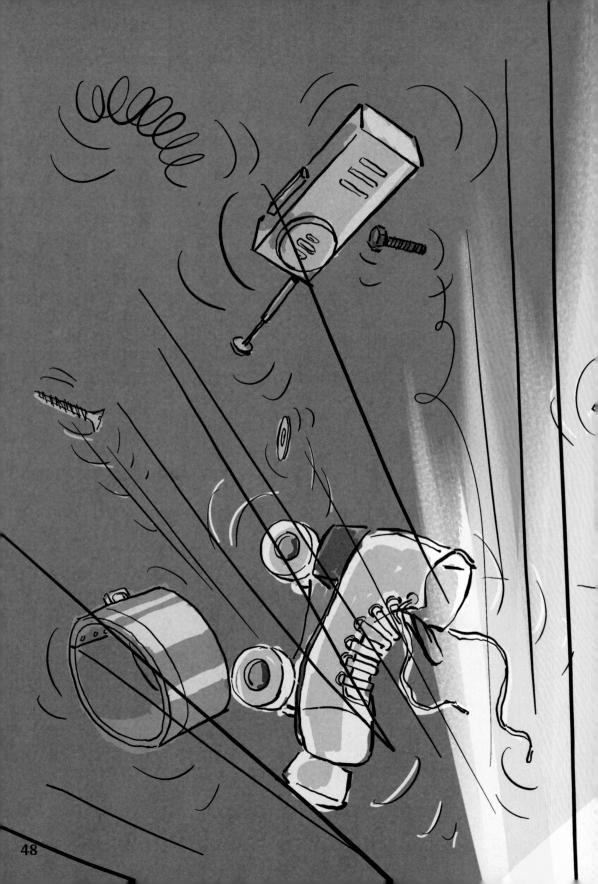

"Bink," said Gollie, "I fear that it will be well-nigh impossible to reconstruct the Stretch-o-Matic."

"Step aside," said Bink. "I'm using my gray matter."

"May I help?" said Gollie.

"Hand me part 22-C," said Bink.

"Now hand me some peanut butter," said Bink.

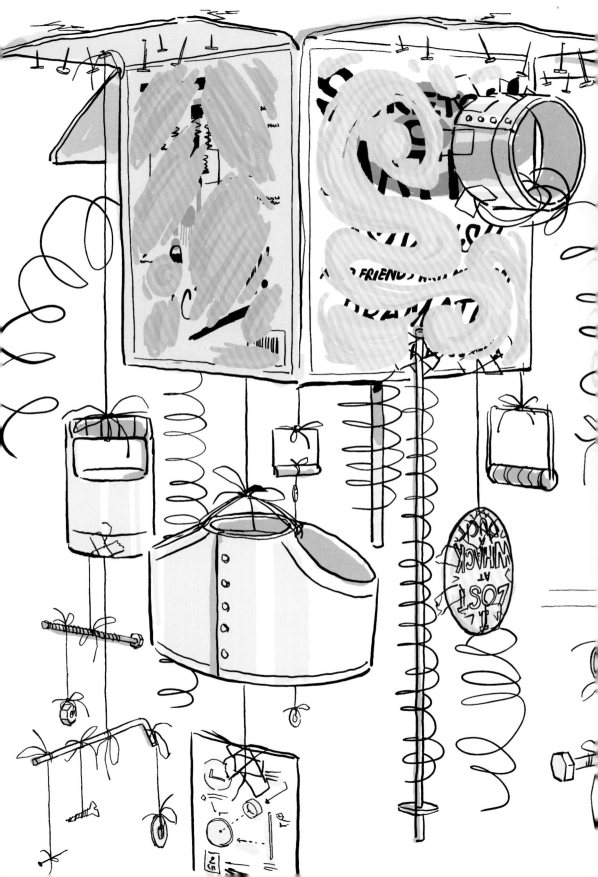

"Astonishing," said Gollie.

"It makes me feel taller just to look at it," said Bink.

"Art can have that effect," said Gollie.

Kudos,

Bink

and

Gollie

"Look, Bink," said Gollie. "Here is Edna O'Dell and her collection of international garden gnomes."

"Hmm," said Bink.

"Look," said Gollie. "Here is the world's largest ball of tinfoil. How very interesting."

"Hmm," said Bink.

"Look," said Gollie. "'Pictured here is Mr. Jerome Gardner of Freeport, New York, sitting with a few million of the marbles in his ever-growing collection. Good work, Jerome.'"

"Hmm," said Bink.

"Maybe we should collect something," said Bink.

"Excellent idea, Bink," said Gollie. "Then we, too, could have our photo in *Flicker's Arcana*."

"But what should we collect?" said Bink.

"Surely we can find something at Eccles' Empire of Enchantment," said Gollie.

"Help you?" said Mr. Eccles.

"Help you?" said Mrs. Eccles.

"Yes," said Gollie. "We would like to start a collection."

"We're going to become world-record holders and get our picture in this book," said Bink.

"Well, as far as collecting goes, you've got your rubber worms," said Mr. Eccles. "You've got your gold star stickers."

"You've got your decorative thimbles," said Mrs. Eccles. "You've got your rings made out of spoons."

"I like gold star stickers," said Bink. "Let's start with gold star stickers."

"Aisle ten," said Mr. Eccles.

"Aisle ten," said Mrs. Eccles.

"One hundred packages of sixty-six stars each makes sixty-six hundred gold star stickers," said Bink. "No one in the entire world could possibly have more gold star stickers than that. We're winners."

"Bink," said Gollie, "I have just made a disturbing discovery. Look: 'Pictured here is Celeste Pascal of Petaluma, California, standing in front of her bungalow, which is entirely covered in gold star stickers. Kudos, Celeste.'"

"Kudos?" said Bink.

"Kudos means congratulations," said Gollie.

"That looks like more than sixty-six hundred gold stars," said Bink.

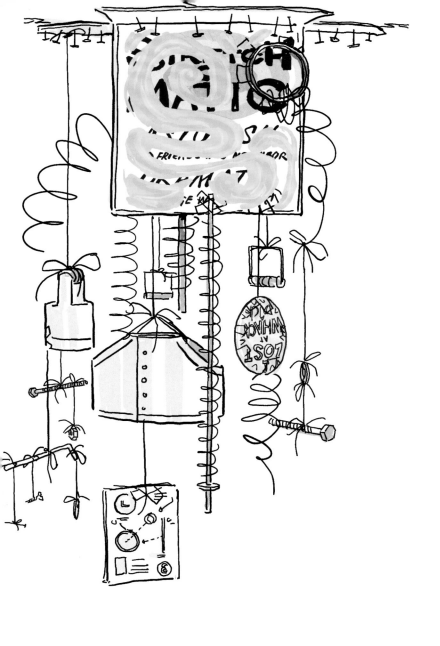

"We don't have a bungalow entirely covered in gold star stickers," said Gollie.

"And we don't have a million marbles," said Bink. "Flicker's will never come to take our picture."

"I can think of someone who would take our picture,"
said Gollie.

"Say cheese," said Mr. Eccles.

"Cheese," said Mrs. Eccles.

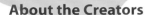

About the Creators

Kate DiCamillo is the author of *The Magician's Elephant*, a *New York Times* bestseller; *The Tale of Despereaux*, which was awarded the Newbery Medal; *Because of Winn-Dixie*, a Newbery Honor Book; and six books starring Mercy Watson, including the Theodor Seuss Geisel Honor Book *Mercy Watson Goes for a Ride*. She lives in Minneapolis.

Alison McGhee is the author of several picture books, including *Song of Middle C*, illustrated by Scott Menchin, and the #1 *New York Times* bestseller *Someday*, illustrated by Peter H. Reynolds; novels for children and young adults, including *All Rivers Flow to the Sea* and the Julia Gillian series; and several novels for adults, including the best-selling *Shadow Baby*, which was a *Today* Book Club selection and was nominated for a Pulitzer Prize. She lives in Minnesota and Vermont.

Tony Fucile is the author-illustrator of *Let's Do Nothing!* and the illustrator of *Mitchell's License* by Hallie Durand. He has spent more than twenty years designing and animating characters for numerous feature films, including *The Lion King*, *Finding Nemo*, and *The Incredibles*. He lives in the San Francisco Bay area.

Praise for the *New York Times* Bestseller
Bink & Gollie

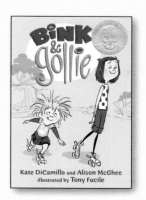

A THEODOR SEUSS GEISEL AWARD WINNER

A *NEW YORK TIMES BOOK REVIEW* BEST ILLUSTRATED CHILDREN'S BOOK OF THE YEAR

• • •

★ "Sharp, distinctly ungirly dialogue makes every page feel like a breath of fresh air . . . inklike digital illustrations crackle with energy and sly humor. . . . Irresistible." — *Publishers Weekly* (starred review)

★ "Witty and earnest . . . expressive and hilarious. . . . More, please!" — *Kirkus Reviews* (starred review)

"Effervescent and endearingly quirky . . . full of zip." — *The Wall Street Journal*

"If you had an All-Star Team for early readers, these three would be in the starting line-up. . . . The characters nearly come alive on the page." — *Chicago Sun-Times*

"An overt love letter to friendship." — *Los Angeles Times*

"Funky and funny." — *Miami Herald*

Another *New York Times* Bestseller
Bink & Gollie: Two for One

A PARENTS' CHOICE RECOMMENDED TITLE

• • •

★ " Readers will delight in sharing their adventures. . . . A funny, touching book." — *School Library Journal* (starred review)

★ "Hits that sweet spot where picture books, graphic novels, and early readers converge. . . . The blend of humor and sympathetic warmth buoys the story throughout. This endearing partnership remains a treat to follow." — *Bulletin of the Center for Children's Books* (starred review)

"A welcome sequel . . . illustrated with zany energy." — *The Wall Street Journal*

"Fucile's lively artwork and detailed cartoon-style drawings, in combination with DiCamillo and McGhee's simple, droll words, are spot-on when it comes to depicting humorous and sympathetic moments, and they excel in highlighting the great joys of best friendship. . . . Completely charming." — *Booklist*